To Maya and Ella and all brown-sugared children of the world. -CWS

Thanks to everyone who raised me up. -A

Boyds Mills Press

An Imprint of Boyds Mills & Kane

boydsmillsandkane.com

Printed in China

ISBN: 978-1-63592-138-0

Library of Congress Control Number: 2019940977

First edition

10 9 8 7 6 5 4 3 2 1

Book Design: Cait Greer

Brown Sugar Babe

by **Charlotte Watson Sherman**

illustrated by **Akem**

BOYDS MILLS PRESS

AN IMPRINT OF BOYDS MILLS & KANE

New York

When you were born, it was dark

behind your sleeping eyes,

blackish-reddish brown

before the grand surprise

when you blinked

and beheld

a world

of color.

"I'm pink,"
you declared
once you grew a tad older.

"Pink," you whispered,

then shouted,

much bolder.

"You're brown like me," I said,

raising your hands to the sun.

"Beautiful, precious brown,

my little one."

"I don't want to be **brown**," said little brown **you**.

"Brown isn't **sunny** or **yummy** or **cute**."

"Brown," I said. "Bubbling brown sugar babe,

honeyed and bright as marmalade."

Your brown eyes are chocolate drops
brown sugar babe

your hair, a crown of brown curls,

fierce as a lion's mane.

Look at those brown legs, sturdy funnels of stone,

your brown arms, wiry and strong as knucklebone.

Stick-around-brown sugar babe.

Brown is silent—

a raisin crinkling in the sun

tree rings that tell time ever since year one

a sand dollar glinting
on the beach in winter

clay turning to mud
after a cloudburst
of rain splinters

our brown hands
clasped tight

when a **zigzag** of lightning strikes.

Brown is loud—

the bassy grumble of ocean waves

rumbling roar of blustery wind

the crunch of peanuts between our teeth

the
squeal
of a violin.

Brown is a desert where copperheads stun.

Brown is a plum spurting sweetness on our tongues.

Brown is dusk
before **day** turns
to twilight.

Brown is **feet**
marching for
human rights.

Brown is a **tutu** and **ballet** slippers poised to **take flight**.

Brown is an **after**-bedtime-story kiss **goodnight.**

Our world is a feast of color,
pink black yellow blue green and red

and **brown** has its own special flavor
like yams, jam, morels, toast, and gingerbread

Brown tastes like **pancakes** and **syrup** and caramel **and** spice

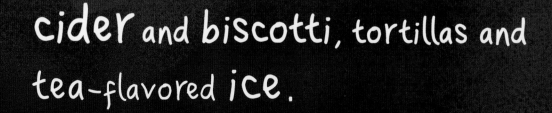

cider and **biscotti**, tortillas and tea-flavored **ice.**

Brown is **soft** as rabbit's **foot** fur.

Brown is **prickly** as porcupette **whiskers**.

Brown smells like pinecones and mulberry bush
woodchips, coffee beans,
and purple asparagus.

Brown is a laughing sound,
raspy and hoarse

fingers snapping, toes tapping, singing and dancing, of course.

Brown is quicksilver.
Brilliant. A fast-moving storm.

Brown is as old as the first star

before even the earth was born.

Brown lasts **forever** like the
roots of this **tree** called **life**

and **our** love,
branches **reaching** toward
the heavens **above**.

"Now, **why** is there anything **else** you'd rather be

besides **brown** sugar babe?" I said.

"Brown like me?"

Author's Note

I love being brown and wanted to write a poem to highlight the splendor of this underestimated color for young boys and girls so they too will love the skin they are in.

When I first heard a beautiful, radiant, brown-skinned child say, "I'm pink," I wondered if she just liked the color pink, or if, even in the New Millennium, brown-skinned children still disbelieved the beauty of their skin. Then I read that the color brown was the least favorite color of Americans. How could that be? The world is chock-full of so much glorious brown.

When the brown-skinned two-year-old declared, "I'm pink," I recalled the doll test conducted as part of the NAACP-led case Brown v. Board of Education. That lawsuit helped the Supreme Court end school segregation in the United States.

In the 1940s, black children could not attend school with white children in many parts of the United States. Psychologists Kenneth and Mamie Clark conducted experiments known as "the doll tests" to study the psychological effects of segregation on African-American children.

The doctors used four dolls, identical except for color, to test racial perceptions. Their subjects, children between the ages of three and seven, were asked to identify both the race of the dolls and which color doll they preferred.

The children were asked which doll was pretty and nice and which was bad. A majority of the girls and boys preferred the white dolls, saying that they were the nice, pretty ones, and the black dolls were bad.

By the time Brown v. Board of Education appeared before the Supreme Court in 1954, the Clarks had collected years' worth of data that led them to conclude "prejudice, discrimination, and segregation" created a feeling of inferiority among African-American children and damaged their self-esteem.

In 2006, 17-year-old New York high school student Kiri Davis made a film entitled A Girl Like Me and recreated the famous 1940 experiment. Ms. Davis wanted to test "how far we've come" in developing positive self-image and self-esteem among brown-skinned children.

Ms. Davis asked the children, "Why do you think this doll is the nice one?"

"Because she's white," the children responded.

"Why do you think this doll is the bad one?"

"Because she's black," the children said. She discovered that we haven't really progressed much, or at all, since the 1940s and 1950s.

However, brown-skinned children with positive brown-skinned role models didn't reject the black dolls. One solution for the issue of low self-esteem among brown-skinned children is to make sure they develop a pro-black identity to protect against the harmful effects of prejudice, discrimination, and segregation. My prayer is that Brown Sugar Babe will help brown-skinned children love the skin they are in.